THE HAUNTING *of* ADDIE LONGWOOD
and OTHER SHORT STORIES

YOLANDA ACKER

Copyright © 2019 Yolanda Acker
All rights reserved
First Edition

PAGE PUBLISHING, INC.
New York, NY

First originally published by Page Publishing, Inc. 2019

ISBN 978-1-68456-294-7 (Paperback)
ISBN 978-1-68456-295-4 (Digital)

Printed in the United States of America

The Haunting of Addie Longwood

Maine, in a town called Ellsworth, where a family moved from sunny California to begin a new life. A twelve-year-old girl named Jessica is blessed with a gift of psychic abilities since her childhood. In a place where no one knew them. Within this small town, a secret was captivated and unraveled into a tale of horror with grim suspense that left everyone in an escapade of awe. In this new town, a girl named Addie Longwood was the most recent victim in a trail of gruesome murders. Psychopathic maniac named Robert Reed who kidnaps twelve-year-old girls to torturing deaths. Jessica meets a girl named Cecilia Stillman who was best friends with Addie. Jessica becomes haunted by the souls of the dead girl's past and her psychic abilities help reveal the killer. The adoring twist of wonderment was when the townspeople of Ellsworth find out the truth that one of their sweet neighbors was a maniac in disguise.

* * *

It rained all day and all night. It was a gloomy end of spring and everyone couldn't wait until summer. Miriam was a very conservative mother, dressed in her casual cream-colored pants and spaghetti-strap blue tank top. She wore plain white sneakers without socks even though it was raining. The humidity was scorching. She wasn't completely pale, but she had an even toned complexion from her weekly hours spent at the tanning salon. Her eyes were a deep-blue and she had this sort of gem in her eyes that enlightened her overall personality. With shoulder-length blond hair she kept well-tapered in a cropped bob. She looked out of the kitchen window dismayed at the weather. She had rescheduled her appointment to view the property in Maine even though they've lived in California since she was a kid. Next week was the day. At least she would have gotten a little bit more packing done. Her house was filled with memories of her own childhood, and she badly needed to break into her own independence.

"Mom! Mom, Jared is being very annoying!" screamed twelve-year-old Jessica in frustration.

Jessica was the oldest of her other two siblings Emmanuel and Jared. Being the only girl made it a little more difficult to deal with the constant sibling rivalries. Lots of times her father tried to make her acknowledge the benefits of being the eldest child. Jessica favored her mother in numerous ways with her blond hair that barely passed her back, her blue eyes, and slender frame. Puberty had already taken its course on her body, and at times, she felt a bit embarrassed as her breasts began to protrude into small nubs. Her mother suggested for her to try using a training bra to make her understand it was part of becoming a woman. The thing she did not yet experience was her period. Miriam regretted the day it would happen. She briefly gazed into her own memory of when she had gotten her package of womanhood. At fourteen, her mother sat her down in a big white chair in the corner of the dining room and began to tell her. She strongly made it clear that it was when you met a man, got married, and had babies of your own. If only mother had sugarcoated the labor pains and struggles of toddlers to adolescents who will eventually turn into adults recycling that same process all over again. Still in all, she carried her mother's words with promise being deceased for nearly six years of cancer. It was the only thing she remembered that actually made sense to her as she got older.

"Okay, let's not continue the day with arguing!" Mom scolded. "When Daddy comes home from work, he's going to be very tired."

Their father had worked long hours in a science lab right on the outskirts of town. He was a real genius creating medicines that cured the most impossible traces of bacteria. Michael Thompson, his name, was known all over Los Angeles. Some of the most prestigious doctors that spent years acquiring knowledge to earn a degree, he gave a ministry of advice to. He earned a nice gross income that greatly allowed his family to engage in trips and some very fine caviar. He was medium built, average height with brown hair, and dark-green eyes. Jared and Emmanuel favored his figure except for Emmanuel having black hair. Both sons took on their father's green eyes as opposed to Jessica. Michael was going to relocate once they moved and already had gotten a position at this high-tech building where he could set up his work. Many of the doctors heard of him, prior to his extensive abilities. In excitement, his future colleagues waited for his arrival. Jared looked at his mother and then turned his head and gave her an apologetic look. She knew he was sorry, so she patted him on the shoulder, and they scurried upstairs to their rooms. It was another hour and Michael would be home. Everyone was almost finished enjoying dinner. Jessica helped her mother clear the table and put the dishes in the dishwasher. Sooner than later, they were fast asleep with Michael arriving any minute. Miriam had just gotten out of the shower and heard the keys jiggle in the lock downstairs.

"Honey, I'm home!" yelled Michael.

He immediately dropped his briefcase by the front door and took off his jacket and tie. He went into the living room and flopped on the recliner and let out a sigh.

Miriam greeted her husband with a hug and long kiss. "Your dinner's in the microwave, honey."

After eating, he took a quick shower. They chatted for a bit, Miriam lay her head on her husband's chest, and they both fell fast asleep.

* * *

It was 3:05 a.m., sirens sounded outside Ellsworth. Another murder had occurred, and the victim was Addie Longwood. Her body was found in the wooded area on Main Street. The girl was kidnapped, raped, and savagely beaten. The neighbors stood in terror watching the coroner pull a lifeless body from the ground. She hadn't even gotten a chance to attend her senior prom or much yet have her first kiss. Addie's parents, George and Nadine Longwood, cried sobbing tears and wailing cries like they were in excruciating pain. Addie's best friend, Cecilia Stillman, was crying too. Cecilia and Addie were best friends since the first grade. Everyone thought they were twins because they both shared the same slender frame, blue eyes, and blond hair. The mind of a madman had taken over in this town for the past fifteen years, and as always, no evidence or semen was matched to anyone they knew. The wind spoke, hollowing and shrieking. On this very day, it seems like there was so much silence in the air. There were no birds chirping and not even a single squirrel sprinting across the maple trees. The police told everyone to clear out of the area and go inside. You never knew if the killer was lurking beside you. Addie's parents went into the sheriff's car to go down to the station. The town sheriff, Mr. James Dunn, had served in Ellsworth for almost twenty years and he never experienced any cases as heinous as this. Addie's mother remembered Cecilia's mom telling her how she offered Addie a ride home after school, but Addie decided to walk. She didn't think of contacting the police until the next day because Addie would usually call the next morning telling her she was at Cecilia's house. Not this time, it was oddly strange though. It couldn't bring back her daughter and if only a careless act like this one would've been something, they all won't be going through now. Addie's mother, Nadine Longwood, vaguely remembered her saying she was going to the Woodlawn Museum after school. Only to get some last minute information on a sculpture for a history report that was due on Friday. Nadine was setting up a meeting on the phone at the time and in between fixing dinner. She shooed Addie away with her hand. Possibly which she knows now, if she had paid attention, she would've picked her up ten minutes earlier. The museum closed at five, so that gave Addie at least two hours to zoom there and be home before getting scolded for her lateness. Addie's father, George Longwood, was crying so hard that his eyes were so swollen. It looked like he was stung by an insect giving him an allergic reaction. Addie's parents were both lawyers and all the most intriguing cases they'd received defending criminals, they felt a sense of hate against the whole law system. Abiding the rules and obstructing boundaries to keep people free to the outside world and more vulnerable to innocent victims like Addie. They had moved to Maine when she was only three months old. Although, it's only now memories of sadness will consume their home. A house right next to theirs had rented owners at least nine times within two years. Coincidentally and oddly strange, all never having children but now there was a for sale sign posted up front. Many of the old neighbors moved in fear of their own lives. Eventually finding out about the tragedy that sustained it. Now the new people would come and relish the horror that claimed Ellsworth. Mr. Darren Marshall was the only neighbor that lived solemnly for the past fifty years. He and his wife, Mabel-Jean, had no real reason to move. They were both retired and neither of them had children. A home for the elderly was not in their preference of living. They enjoyed summer nights sitting on the porch, sipping lemonade, and watching the moon fall almost yet peacefully before the murders began, that's all they tried to remember. They were a very well-reserved couple and knew each and every neighbor that lived in Ellsworth. Watching the children grow up but feared the day they'd have to reveal the truth to someone they barely knew. Even the mere suspense of expecting one of the children to fathom this horror. Robert Reed was a guy Darren had grown to dislike. A local painter who had done various odd jobs for folks allowed him to fashion his reputation quite respectfully. Mabel didn't have a problem with him. She actually thought he was a nice guy trying to make an honest living. Darren seemed rather bothered by her comment. Ever since he was a young boy, he had been able to feel good and bad off other people's auras. This was a secret only he and his wife had shared.

  Knowing how the murders spun in patterns, he didn't feel this person had reason to attack them. Hell…they had no children, so that was the least of their worries. Yet in still, he felt pain for the ones that were caught as his victims. Robert Reed had the sincerest charm, but he also took on a character that was an artificial one. He had some sort of degree in art, so he was definitely recognized for being witty and articulate. He made a very decent living out of this and at one occasion or another. The biggest lawyer from Washington who had briefly visited Maine to pay his respects to his sister's deceased husband gratefully paid him ten thousand dollars just to draw an upscale high rise in the center of his living room wall. The lawyer, Ed Graham, was keen on perfection, and he had this flare for creativity. What did you expect for someone as polished as he was. Not to care a flying fuck how much it cost just as long as it was what he wanted. Anyhow, whenever these murders occurred, Robert always seemed to make an unexpected appearance right around the time when local authorities are doing their sweep of names and onlookers that might have any kind of details or clues. As always, *nothing*.

After a while, approximately a week after Addie's murder, he just disappeared. He probably had just gotten tired of the confusion and such, nor did he have any children or close relatives to leave behind. He had often spoke about moving to a much quieter place. He lived on the other side of town, and it was just working people who spent their spare time sipping lattes and planning trips to Cancun during the summer. He had traveled New York City for some months and even thought of getting an apartment in Greenwich Village, but still, it wasn't the reason he decided to come back to Ellsworth.

* * *

"I can't believe it's already two weeks," Miriam told her husband.

The whole family had gotten up early for moving day. It was 7:00 a.m. and breakfast was already on the table. Mom's French toast was a tradition of the Johansen family. Eggs and sausages were being placed onto plates while Jared filled everyone's glasses with orange juice. It seemed so normal for silence during breakfast until dinner. Maybe if they ate more in between meals together, they wouldn't fight so much.

"Mom, is this where we're going to live until I go to college?" asked Emmanuel.

He sometimes studied more on the outcome of things while Jessica and Jared just went along with whatever decision their parents decided.

"Well, actually, I was hoping so. Once the fall comes and you guys enroll in school, you'll get to like it more meeting friends," Miriam explained.

Throughout the remainder of breakfast, everyone was quiet. Jessica had her own thoughts cramming her mind but didn't want to speak about it to her mother. She knew how the moving was sort of supposed to make some kind of change in her life, so she didn't want her mother to feel disappointed. Last night she had the most terrible dream. It was an occasional thing for her. When she was five years old, she would have the strangest visions—seeing ghosts. Only to be diagnosed as it being her imagination by her personal psychiatrist. Her name was Ms. Louise V. Tanner. She was a chunky sized woman in her early forties and had no children which made it awfully confusing to Jessica. How was it so easy for her to get into her head without having any practice besides a piece of paper stating that. Jessica wasn't aware that most people with occupations like this had to go to school. Not the normal freshman to senior but many years of a school called college. Being only twelve, there were still a lot of things ahead of her to know and she had no idea what was before her. When her parents began to notice her behavior, they recommended she see a psychiatrist until the phase, as they called it, began to stop. From the age of five until her ninth birthday, it seemed to have completely vanished. She had no ghostly encounters, she felt normal. To her mother and father, it was just some stage they knew would eventually pass. Wondering why it came back again was a fear she dreaded. If her parents knew, she thought they'd probably try to lock her up in some kind of caged asylum with other children her age. Possibly giving them doses of nasty tasting medicines that erased your memories and put you to sleep. Miriam cleared the table, and everyone went upstairs to retrieve their luggage. Dad had already hired interior decorators to furnish the whole house two weeks to four weeks before they arrived there. A blue minivan was parked outside the driveway—this was the family's only vehicle. Besides the gold Mercedes, their father had traded in to downsize their living expenses. It held pretty roughly with the traveling and good mileage. It was something that would probably be passed down to Jessica when she turned sixteen and learned how to drive. Knowing simply of the offer, she would most likely want a new one. Jessica sat in the back, by the window, and the boys usually took their same spots in the third-row section seats. They all prepared for the drive with sodas and snacks and there was even a disc player installed in the headrest for movies. It was always fun traveling because it gave family time a bit more excitement, since everyone was so tied up during the week with other activities. Dad got in the driver's seat and started the engine. The streets were barely empty. Usually, at this time of morning on a Saturday, most of the neighbors stayed asleep until ten or eleven. Jessica spotted one of her friends from middle school. A brunette-haired girl that she knew since fourth grade. They talked casually but only just became close friends two years ago. She had her number, and they called each other almost every day. She promised to let her visit during the weekends and some holidays once they settled into their new house. She talked for a moment and hugged her goodbye and then decided to text her in between the ride. She was the only one that had a cell phone. She felt important and independent. It was a form of privacy she had from her brothers. Peeking in her diary and exposing her most secret and intimate crushes. Michael pulled out of the driveway and drove smoothly onto the highway. A few hours past and once they arrived at the intersection, the traffic seemed a little more clear. Michael was able to notch up his speed. Miriam had fallen asleep and Emmanuel and Jared were still fascinated, gazing at the sights driving by. They had watched four movies and skimmed through two comic books. Michael eventually stopped at a nearby gas station at least three miles ahead of Maine. Miriam woke up and saw the rest stop and everyone quickly got out and stretched. They all walked into the little store attached to the gas station called Mr. Pop's Deli. Gas wasn't the only thing they needed right now. The boys walked down the small, cramped isles and looked at the items curiously. Jessica got a Coca-Cola and a turkey-and-cheese subsandwich that was premade and wrapped in plastic. Miriam noticed that the boys couldn't decide on anything, so she got everyone else subsandwiches too. Michael placed drinks, chips, and some chocolate-chip cookies on the counter. As Michael paid the cashier for the items with his credit card, he was too busy to notice the strange man that was staring at Jessica. Jessica was standing behind her father near the counter and consciously glanced back. The man looked at her with hungry eyes. He wore some faded jeans and a white T-shirt with some paint stains smeared on it. Maybe he was a painter, she thought, on his lunch break. Even still, the way his eyes followed hers made her uncomfortable and a bit creepy. She quickly rushed out of the store to the van. After that, for some odd reason, she had a vision of a girl being tortured to death. Her palms were sweaty, and she felt dizzy. She took a sip of the water that she had earlier in the cooler on the side of her seat. She put the water bottle down and laid her head back.

"Maine...another three and a half miles," Michael announced.

Jessica closed her eyes and went to sleep.

Addie's parents was preparing for the funeral. Addie wore a cotton white frilled dress, and her skin was pale and taken. It was a quick ceremony, everyone paying respects and some old friends of her mother from high school that followed each other straight out of law school. It was a shame that this happened. Everyone that knew her was feeling like she was so lucky to have parents like she did. She never knew what it was like to see her parents argue about the slightest thing. For the most part, Addie's parents suggested friends and family wear dark-colored attire. The depressing appearance seemed to worsen the whole outlook on her death. There was no one saying, "Oh, she's in heaven now." Just a room full of tears wondering how could this happen. The reception of food and drinks were immediately set after. All the food was neatly arranged by the caterer's menu of appetizers and wine. As fast as her father wanted the pain to go away, the longer people lingered around would just make him more tense. After a half an hour, hugs were given, and shoulders were patted. With soothing words like "Everything will be all right." Which was the typical compliment you'd expect to hear. When if it was all right, this funeral wouldn't even be taking place after all. Cars parked outside next to two limousines sped away with brief waves of goodbye. It was not too long when the house was back to normal, except for that emptiness left in Addie's room. It sort of felt like she was just away at college for the time being and will be reunited with her parents during spring break. Those were just mere thoughts of what they both wished. The denial had sunken in very deep, and it might take a few more days, even months to realize she was gone forever. Nadine took another look in her daughter's room. She walked in and sat down across her bed. She started sobbing for a minute, thinking of her daughter lying next to her. She felt a cold drift of air brush past her very lightly. Nadine looked around the room to see if the window was open, but it was closed. She got up and tried to think nothing of it. Perhaps the window was cracked just a little. She stood up and walked toward the window to double check, and surely, it was sealed shut. Still puzzled by it, Nadine figured she was probably imagining it. It was stupid and senseless to ponder on what it could have been, after all. The death of her only child was beginning to cause mild hallucinations as per her psychiatrist's diagnosis. She went into the bathroom and showered and then took a nap. Her husband went for a quick run into town to the dry cleaners and the antique shop to get Addie's shoes bronzed, the ones she had worn as an infant. He went upstairs into his bedroom and walked over to his wife, gently kissing her on the cheek. She was already asleep, and he didn't want to wake her. He hurried downstairs and went out the front door. The car they owned was a very classic Mercedes, black with all the detailed interior. George stood in silence for a moment, feeling the coldness of Addie's presence was all too wretched to fathom. George opened the door and proceeded to the driver's seat of his car. As he drove into town, a sort of calmness came over him. The sort of calm feeling you get during a tragedy knowing that something good will come out of it. He never really had any kind of religious beliefs, although, he, at times, did think there was a spirit god. Nadine and George had attended church a few times, even gotten Addie blessed. What difference did it make now since she was dead, or maybe now her young soul would go to that place they called heaven and rest peacefully watching over them. Nadine and George were not the type of people you'd see on the news about parents killing their child for a million dollars. Even simply hiring an ex-con to kidnap their child and proposition the town mayor to help pay for the ransom. They were descent people living a normal life. It was so odd and so very careless. Such a devilish act committed by someone who was probably sipping coffee and watching rerun episodes of MASH. George stopped at the corner waiting for the red light to turn green. After two minutes of waiting, he made a left turn and parked in front of the dry cleaners. He let out a sigh of disappointment before walking into the shop. The woman who greeted George knew him and his wife all the time they had lived in Maine. George liked how they had specially tailored his suits for him a day before his big cases, a crisp look from spritzes of cornstarch. He had also referred some of his best colleagues to also dry-clean there. It was only three cleaners in their town of which this was the most popular. The woman was Mrs. Gloria Pine Hill and her husband, Rue, shared the responsibility of the work. They were both in their early fifties, and they were plain looking people's business and just watched. Gloria and her husband had three children who lived in Wisconsin. Her children paid her a holiday visit every Thanksgiving and Christmas. Her two oldest sons, Paul and Mackie, did some type of overseas stock investment. This made them both happy to know that their children had earned a good life for themselves. George thought of the time when Addie was alive, opening gifts on Christmas day. When Mrs. Pine Hill and her husband heard the news about Addie's death, they cried like she was one of their own. Such a sweet girl, they knew her as, yet so easily open to the whims of this killer still lurking around somewhere. George gave Mrs. Pine Hill the yellow receipt slip that she needed to get his finished tailoring. He had two grey business suits, a white long-sleeved collared shirt and three pairs of slacks that needed hemming. She took the receipt and went toward the back to pick up the items. George carefully watched her sift through the plastic from other clothing hanging, and he saw Mr. Pine Hill at the left corner using an iron to crease a woman's skirt. The cleaners smelled of starch and the mist from the heat from the ironing made it very hot inside. George was getting agitated and hoped to leave in a hurry. Mrs. Pine Hill quickly returned to the counter with George's clothes. They were neatly placed on a wire hanger with a piece of plastic covering it.

"That will be thirty-six dollars, please," she said.

He pulled out a fifty-dollar bill and told her to keep the change. He quickly left the shop and was feeling thirsty after standing inside for so long. He was sweating on his neck and the palms of his hands. George decided to keep his car parked in the parking space and walked over to the antique shop, two doors down. Passing an ice-cream shop, he remembered how much Addie loved vanilla ice cream with caramel sundae topping. A man from inside the parlor waved at George as he passed by. George waved back. He reached the antique shop and walked inside. The man who had worked there, Mr. Leonardis, what everyone called him, had his shop for over twenty years. He was born in Russia and came here to Maine. He had bought some of the finest antique pieces to Ellsworth and the people and tourists, as well, loved them. After a while, it grew boring and more people just went to the local malls. Only the tourists or new neighbors found this shop fascinating. Mr. Leonard was a short, stocky old man. His hair was balding, and he always kept an intense look on his face. He lived in Maine for at least eight years before he left Switzerland. When the murders began, he thought if this person was living in his country at the time when he was a kid, how gruesome his punishment would have been. George took Addie's shoes out of the small, white box he was carrying. The shoes were an off-white trimmed with pink. He told Mr. Leonard how he wanted them bronzed and said he would pick it up next week. Nadine was going to put them in a glass case and display it on a shelf in their living room next to Addie's picture. George left the store and walked a bit quickly to his car. He felt the tears start to fall from the corners of his eyes. He wanted to get home to his wife and hold her very tightly.

* * *

The blue minivan pulled up to the big white house on the corner. It seemed so much bigger than their old house in California. With an attic and a finished basement, it would be more than enough adventures for Jared and Emmanuel to create.

"Wow, this place is huge!" said Jared excitedly.

They both ran to the front of the house with Emmanuel opening the door with the keys his mother gave him. Jessica looked around the neighborhood and saw no one but a blond-haired girl jumping rope. She waved hi to Jessica, and Jessica waved back.

"See, honey, you're starting to make friends already," her mother said with a warm smile.

Jessica shrugged her shoulders and went inside the house. Michael stepped back out for a moment to remove the for-sale sign from the porch.

"Don't need this anymore."

Soon after everyone was inside, they began viewing the whole house. Opening bedroom doors, gasping with their oohs and ahhs. This was really the first time they had seen it besides on pictures from the website. The realtor offered them a great deal, and they accepted on such short notice. The realtor told them the history of the town and prove Maine would be worth the move. The landmark itself was very historical. The lighthouses were the best sights to see, especially at night. Jessica chose the master bedroom on the second floor next to the attic. She felt happy and serene knowing that she will finally have some privacy away from her annoying brothers. The best thing about the house was that the furniture was already displayed when Miriam ordered everything. Jessica's bedroom set was an off-white with a French canopy bed. She felt like a queen in her own world. The family sat down in the dining room for pizza, cheesy breadsticks, and soda. Night came so quickly. Emmanuel had packed two neon glow sticks he had won at a school fair in California. He gave one to Jared. They were already inventing fun in their new room, laughing, and talking about some kind of tree house they were going to ask their father to build in the backyard. After a while, they fell asleep. Michael and Miriam were both asleep too. Jessica was relaxing in her bed. She had kept a small butterfly night light on that she had since she was two years old. It was hard for her to go to sleep if the room was completely dark. She watched the shadows on the walls play tag. She never liked to sleep in total darkness because the visions used to frighten her so much as a child. For some reason, it was hard for her to fall asleep at this moment. It was something keeping her awake. Suddenly she had the urge to pee. She got out of bed and put on her pink, fuzzy rabbit slippers. She turned on the light aitch next to the door. Looking at herself in the mirror, she was ashamed to see how frizzy her hair was. She went to her nightstand and got her brush. Looking back in the mirror, she brushed her hair down and placed the brush on the edge of the sink. She stared for a moment and thought it was her visions coming back to haunt her again. A girl, around her age, stared back at her in the mirror with cold, sad eyes. She had blond hair, and she looked badly beaten from the scars that were across her face. Jessica whimpered almost softly hoping no one would hear her. She closed her eyes tight and prayed that the face disappeared when she opened her eyes again. *It did.*

This was a feeling she knew wouldn't go away. She got back in her bed and shut her eyes, not caring about anything else. Jessica had a way of fear purposely putting her to sleep. If she hadn't seen the girl, maybe she'd still be awake thinking of how tired she was. She drifted into a deep dream of roses, and a garden filled with flowers. When she awoke from this fantasy, she realized it was six in the morning. She turned the knob on the back of the alarm clock that was sat on her nightstand to shut off the buzzing sound. It was Sunday, and she deserved an extra hour or two after the weird experience she had last night. The smell of coffee was brewing downstairs, and Michael usually prepared a cup for himself and Miriam. Michael went upstairs and gave Miriam her cup of coffee while he sat in bed slowly sipping his. He thought of just letting the boys sleep all the way until twelve. That would be a first because for the past three years our Sundays were devoted to social outings for charities. The quiet time they had now was well appreciated.

Jessica tossed and turned and woke up in a mild sweat. Her hair was matted down to the nape of her neck and she felt a bit nauseated. She decided to get up and go downstairs for some breakfast. She rushed into the bathroom to wash her face and brush her teeth. She washed her face with cold water, she needed that. She figured if she had eaten something then she would feel a little bit better. She casually glanced out of her bedroom window before heading downstairs. It was someone at the front door. By the time she reached the stairs, her mother was already greeting an unfamiliar man. A man almost her father's height, stood looking calmly with dark-brown hair and green eyes. Jessica gave him a suspicious glare, thinking she might have seen him somewhere before.

"Hello, neighbors, my name is Robert Reed. I'm the local painter roun' this part of town." He held out his hand and gestured for Miriam to give him a handshake.

Just then Michael walked out of the kitchen and greeted him too. Miriam gave him a quick smile and silently thought to herself that he was fairly handsome. She looked away feeling ashamed. Robert looked at Jessica, and it gave her an eerie, uncomfortable feeling.

"Now who might this pretty young lady be?" he asked.

"This is Jessica, our oldest child. We also have two sons. We're from California," Michael addressed.

"Well, if you ever need any work done, I'm the handyman around here, everyone knows me." He handed Michael a white business card with his name and phone number on it.

Michael gave his thanks and even asked if he would come over sometime and have a cold beer. That was a bad idea so to speak. Michael smiled and closed the door. Jessica peeked at the neighbor from the kitchen window. Watching him walk down a dirt road to wherever he was going. She saw that girl again, who lived across the street. She saw her standing in her garage because obviously the garage door was open. Her and another woman who resembled the girl, which was probably her mother, was pulling items out of the garage and placed them on a long wooden table in their front yard. The girl walked out with a cardboard sign that said GARAGE SALE.

Jessica went into the kitchen to make herself a quick bowl of cereal. Her parents had gone back upstairs, she was alone in the kitchen now. After a short time, her two brothers were coming down the stairs with her father.

"On our way to walk to the bakery. Jess, wanna come?" her father asked.

"No, thanks, I might check out the yard sale going on." Jessica went upstairs and had a cold shower.

She threw on some pink shorts, a T-shirt, and her sneakers. She brushed her hair into a ponytail and headed across the street. The girl was standing near some knickknacks that was on another table and looked up at Jessica.

"Hi, my name is Cecilia."

"Hi, my name is Jessica. I'm from California. We moved into that white house over there."

Cecilia was very pretty. She wore her hair hanging down with a yellow headband. She had sandals that Jessica never seen before. The fashion of Maine was so nondescriptive.

"Hello, you're the new neighbors, huh?" her mother asked, walking toward Cecilia with another load of things.

"Well, I'm Glenda, and this is my daughter whom I see you've already met."

Cecilia's father, James, was also in the garage lifting a heavy recliner that had a small tear on the left side. He waved hello, letting one arm loose, then continued carrying it to the curb. He sat it down and wiped his forehead with a blue handkerchief.

"Whew, that's heavy, I can't remember the last time I sat in that thing!"

Glenda introduced her husband to Jessica. He looked at Jessica and then glanced at Cecilia.

"You remind me of Cecilia's best friend, Addie, she was murdered a few months ago." He made a sad expression and walked back in the garage.

Cecilia gave her father an angry look. Her father sure had a way with being outspoken. After that remark, Jessica felt disturbed and eerie. She felt her head spinning and saw a picture of the man with the faded jeans with the paint stains on it during the time they went to the rest stop before they arrived here. Cecilia's mother asked Jessica if she was all right and offered her a glass of lemonade. She came back with a huge glass and Jessica gulped it down very quickly, suddenly feeling very thirsty. She asked if she could help them, and Cecilia and Jessica began arranging items on the wooden table. Miriam caught sight from the living room window and walked over to introduce herself as well. Before long the two women sprung into a conversation like they had known each other for years. Suddenly the blue minivan was turning into their driveway.

"Oh, that must be my husband and two sons."

What an unexpected gathering, everyone talking and laughing. Glenda invited them inside, and they all shared lemonade and chocolate-chip cookies. Emmanuel and Jared gave Cecilia a hard stare. They went inside and started sketching their own blueprint for their treehouse. Jessica and Cecilia stood outside as the other neighbors crowded around the table. Cecilia introduced Jessica to everyone, and it seemed like this Addie-girl was very well-liked. Many of them looked with surprised faces and made comments about how she resembled Addie so much. Maybe that's why Cecilia had taken a liking to her so fast. She did mention that she and Addie were also best friends. Jessica felt some kind of bond between them and suddenly a dark gloom swept past her shoulders. She looked back to see if it was one of her brothers playing around, but it was only Mr. Robert Reed that was behind her. He stared at her with those cold eyes again. All of a sudden, the yard sale was filled with half the neighbors of Ellsworth.

"Hey, I know you!" Robert screamed loudly to Jessica.

Everyone turned around a looked with puzzled faces. "You're Addie Longwood coming back to haunt me!"

The neighbors looked like they had seen a ghost. When it was really Robert Reed who had thought Jessica was one. Suddenly a ghost did appear, right behind Robert Reed. It was Addie Longwood. Just then Addie's parents had been driving by and got out to view the yard sale, and another neighbor whispered to them what was going on. It was her, Addie, standing there next to Robert Reed. Her body was completely bloody, and her face looked old and decrepit. She was so sad with dark eyes. Her clothes were torn apart and she had the most awful smell you could ever imagine. Jessica couldn't believe her eyes. She saw Addie, too, and so did everyone else. There was gasps of fear amongst the crowd and her parents began to cry. This was the same girl she had seen in the mirror last night, the same presence she felt around her. At this point, Robert was in a state of paranoia. He thought his sanity was starting to get the best of him. He stood there in a state of confession explaining in detail one by one, all his victims he had killed, including Addie Longwood. Everyone was in utter shock, Addie's mother fainted, and her husband immediately called the ambulance. Cecilia's mother went inside and phoned the police. Boy, was this going to make headlines.

"We got him. The murderer who killed Addie!"

Seconds later, the police arrived, grabbing Robert Reed handcuffing him very tight. The cop shoved him in the back seat of the car and slammed the door, driving off furiously. He was not sentenced to life but death. In his own hell, he will be forever tortured by the souls of the victims and their ghosts. The worst was over, and the town of Ellsworth was able to rest peacefully. You see, the only mystery was to find the truth and save the town from this evil, and the truth has set them free.

For the Love of Dolls

She had taken a great liking to Fallow. Her authenticity was genuine, and her name was signed neatly on the heel of her ceramic foot. She wore a red velvet dress with white lace trimmings on the edges. Her hair reached her back and it was the darkest you'd ever seen. Her eyes were motionless, as her carved lips were painted in a soft pink, and her eyelashes were made of the finest Indian hairs. She was just shipped from Taiwan, and Peculiar loved her. She had others, but this one was her very favorite. The little bell hanging at the top of the door rang, and Peculiar looked up from the counter.

"Hello, I was wondering if you can engrave initials on this doll for me, please. It's for my little cousin's birthday," the woman stated, pointing at the porcelain doll in her hand.

It was very original with a plain white dress, white stockings, and black patent leather shoes. The woman was very well-dressed in her satin skirt with a blue knitted top bearing her cleavage only slightly. She was a customer that often came into the shop to get extra details on old antiques, but this was the first time she bought in a doll.

"Oh, okay, I will have it engraved for you now if you wish," said Peculiar.

"Oh, I'm sort of in a hurry, but I will pick it up in the morning. The birthday party is tomorrow afternoon." The lady left a twenty-dollar bill on the counter and quickly walked out of the shop.

Peculiar was a very timid woman. She had family back in Idaho but rarely kept in touch, only brief calls during the holidays and such. She had chestnut-brown hair and dark-brown eyes. Peculiar was once married but her husband recently died from natural causes. She bore no children, but yet, she had a childlike image about her. She was always fascinated by dolls ever since she could remember. She opened her own little shop called "Peculiar's Dolls and Things" with the money that was left to her from her husband's insurance. She was able to live off his earnings and made a collection of dolls her hobby. Peculiar also had a talent for making them. In the oddest form, she was able to create images of these dolls to be whatever the customers wanted. Many people from other parts of town came in with pictures of deceased loved ones, and Peculiar made the warmth of love embedded into longtime memories for each of them. She owned a small cottage-like house just a mile away from her shop, and she drove to work every morning in her grey convertible. She was not too keen on fashion, she wore mostly long skirts and buttoned-up blouses and kept her hair pulled back in a neat bun. Behind her glasses she looked like she was in her midforties, but she was barely thirty. All the dolls were placed on shelves looking lifeless yet so real. Many of them were created by hand by Peculiar. It was only Fallow that was not originally hers. Fallow was special, and Peculiar had a special place for her. She talked to these dolls, and they often talked back. Small whispers clouded the air inside the shop and only Peculiar could hear them. They had conversations of secrets and untold lies that drowned the sorrows of the people they were familiar to. South Carolina was a place where many ancestors relived. It was the power of the very souls that kept them coming back. It was almost time for Peculiar to take her midday break. It was now 11:00 a.m. and she decided to take a walk to the small restaurant across the street for something to eat. She put on her beige shawl covering her arms, then she grabbed her keys from the hook hanging by the cash register. It was nearly fall, and the leaves were falling in orange and red. The brisk air swept through the open window of the shop and made Peculiar shiver just a little. She opened the cash register and took out a ten-dollar bill. As she closed it, she heard a light murmur from one of the dolls on the shelf. She looked at them with sad eyes.

"Don't worry, my sweets, I will only be a little while." She managed a weak smile and locked the door behind her.

The restaurant was crowded today, not more than usual. People sat at square tables end enclosed themselves in the booths that were by the windows. Each table was neatly arranged with napkin holders and salt and pepper shakers sitting on top of red plastic tablecloths. Peculiar picked her regular seat at the far end corner. Lucky for her, this time it wasn't occupied, or she'd have to sit amongst the noisy folks. The ones who talked loudly and had grease stains smeared on their mouths from hamburgers and fries. She hated the stares she often got from people. Although she was known in the town for her beautiful sculptured dolls, some of them felt she was a bit strange. Never mind that because Peculiar had a surprise for all of them, soon enough. A young-looking girl with a red apron approached the table.

"How are you today, miss? What will you be having, our brunch special?" the young waitress asked Peculiar.

The brunch special consisted of toasted grilled-cheese sandwich, with chicken noodle soup, and tea or coffee. The side appetizer was a small Caesar salad.

"Yes, as a matter of fact, I will have that today," Peculiar answered with a warm smile.

The young waitress scribbled down the order on a pink slip of paper and nibbled on the end of the pencil as she waited for Peculiar to decide if she wanted anything else. She gave her the bill and headed toward the kitchen to place the order. Peculiar sat at the table gazing out the window across from her. A fat man with gray hair was approaching the restaurant and walked over to the red-haired cashier at the counter. They were talking and laughing, and suddenly, the lady nodded her head to the man and came back with a cup of coffee and something that might have been home fries with scrambled eggs. The man chewed with his mouth open, still talking and laughing with the lady. Peculiar knew him very well, although, she despised him very much. About three years ago before her husband died, he had threatened to withhold all of her husband's earnings because he had owed a small sum of money for a fine. The fine was generally due to the insufficient maintenance of their yard. During the time, her husband became sick, and it was extremely difficult to tend to the animals they had once owned and tended to. The Department of Health felt the conditions were unsanitary. It was legal to own a farm but illegal to fail the inspection. At that time, they were selling produce and meat at the local farmer's market, and it was giving them a huge financial gain. They ended up taking the animals as partial payment, and the balance was agreed to be paid by confiscating anything else they had owned. The fat man, Mr. Newman Grace, was the owner of the Department of Health in their town. He told Peculiar that the amount would continue to increase until the payments were made. When he found out that her husband had died, he put the full responsibility on Peculiar. Ever since she had her shop, he had occasionally reminded her to pay and threatened to shut down her place. She never really took it into consideration because he always stayed out of town, so she thought she had enough time. When he returned, she only feared the worst. The young girl came back with a large tray and sat it on Peculiars table. The girl gave Peculiar a half smile and walked away. As she ate her food, she thought about Fallow and how lonely she must be. She didn't want to rush, so she tried to enjoy her food and just hoped the dolls would be safe. As she began to take her last bite of her grilled-cheese sandwich, she looked up and saw Mr. Newman Grace approaching her table. Her heart raced and she swallowed what was left of her sandwich. Looked up with a weak smile.

"Hello, Peculiar, I haven't seen you in quite some time. You know you're way overdue. I'll be seeing you around." He slapped a white receipt folded in half on the table next to her tray.

He walked away with an evil sneer on his face, leaving the restaurant full and satisfied. Peculiar unfolded the receipt. The receipt had said that she had to pay twenty thousand dollars in one lump sum in two weeks. If the amount was not paid on time in full, then Mr. Newman Grace will close down her shop. She began to feel tears trickle down the side of her cheek. This was all she had, all she owned after her leaving her unexpectedly. She wiped her eyes and looked around the restaurant hoping no one was paying attention. Everyone was engaging in conversations while they ate. She left a ten-dollar bill on the table for the waitress. She hurried out the door before anyone could notice her. She couldn't believe how heartless he was, even knowing that her husband was no longer around. Mr. Grace had been so inconsiderate of her feelings. She knew it would eventually come to this point, even though it hurt, she felt she was ready now.

She walked into the shop and saw the dolls were still in place. They looked at her with lonely eyes, and she felt they knew something was wrong.

"He's coming to destroy us, and we will be separated. I will never see you again my friends!" she sobbed.

The dolls let out whispers of sadness, and Fallow turned her head and looked at Peculiar. For years, she had instilled love into their hearts that made them finally come alive. She often recited a chant every night before she closed.

"The day you speak I shall hear your voice, the day you move will be time to take vengeance of my choice. This solemn prayer I secretly span, you are in my control I have created you from the devil's hand!"

She sprinkled some white dust over the dolls for protection, turned off the light. On her way out, a customer walked in, it was a mother and her child. The woman looked around and asked Peculiar if she carried doll clothing. Peculiar said no and the lady immediately left the shop. Peculiar went to the front door of the shop and turned the sign on the door to say: BE BACK IN A MINUTE.

She decided to start on what was left of her project. She couldn't waste any more time. Mr. Grace was surely going to get his pay, but unfortunately for him, it wasn't going to be in cash. She took a big cardboard box from underneath the shelf near the register and placed each doll carefully in it. One by one, they looked at her while their tiny lips quivered as she laid them facedown.

One of the dolls asked her very quietly, as soft as a mosquito buzzing in her ear, "Where are you taking us, Peculiar?"

She didn't answer the doll named Sophia. The boy dolls just watched her with frowned faces. Once they were all in the box, she headed to the basement of the shop to perform her ceremony. She opened the basement door and with the key she had taken from the little gold box near the front door upstairs she turned the lock gently. The lock twisted and made a drilling sound. She carried the box of dolls downstairs. The steps creaked, and the dolls turned over, moving and gurgling frightening cries. She sat the box next to a large mat on the floor with white candles surrounding them. She waited for the dolls to become calm, and one by one, they each made their way out of the box and next to Peculiar. Fallow stood in front of her, and Peculiar placed her in her lap, sitting cross-legged in the middle of a rug. She began to explain to them how Mr. Grace was going to take the shop. She told them if they wanted her to be with them forever, they had to cooperate in helping her work. The dolls nodded in agreement and waited patiently for her order. Peculiar stood up with Fallow in her hand and recited the chants she had done every night before she closed. The dolls looked at her and started smiling devilish laughs in unison. A gust of wind waved over the dolls and Peculiar. A large puff of white smoke billowed above them. The basement grew dark, and more white smoke billowed the area, finally leaving them in total darkness. Silence fell, and there were no more whispers or voices. Everything was still and quiet. The night came suddenly.

The next morning was very busy. A few people passed by Peculiar's shop but were disappointed to find that she was out with a sign on the front door that read: BE BACK IN A MINUTE. The woman that had promised to come back for her relative's doll was also puzzled. Unlike the other customers, disregarding the sign, she turned the knob on the front door and walked in. She looked around hoping to see Peculiar standing at the register, but no one was there. She walked closer to the counter and rambled around the store. She had remembered seeing the shelf behind the counter filled with dolls standing with blank faces. Now they were all gone. She began to get frustrated at how Peculiar had also promised to have the initials engraved on the doll today for the birthday party. She took out a piece of paper from her purse and borrowed the pen that was on the counter.

The note said, "Please give me a refund!"

She placed the pen back on the counter and furiously walked out of the shop. The door slammed, and the little bell that was hanging at the top broke off and crumbled into small pieces on the floor.

The day came and went, and it was night again. The shop was still empty and no longer occupied by Peculiar. Many of the customers started to wonder if the shop was closed down for good. Two weeks later and the shop was still empty. Mr. Newman Grace was fuming with anger. He had distinctly warned Peculiar that if she did not respond in time to his request, he would surely have her shop permanently shut down. Mr. Grace hopped into his blue Mercedes and drove quickly to Peculiar's shop. He was in such a hurry that his wheels scratched the ground when he made an abrupt stop at the door. He saw the sign and was too upset to care if she was there or not. He pushed the door open and walked in. He looked around and saw no one. He walked over to the counter and saw the note that the woman had left. He started to wonder if she may have skipped town. He had wondered what happened to the dolls and suspected she had taken them with her too. He walked around the register toward the far end of the shop and seen that the basement door was partially open. He flicked on the light switch and crept downstairs. He couldn't believe what he saw. It was the strangest sight and yet it confused him very much. All the dolls were standing in a circle, and Fallow stood in the middle surrounded by them. Suddenly the basement grew cold. A gust of white smoke appeared, and a flash of light shot around Mr. Newman Grace. The basement became dark and it was quiet once again. The lady who had left the note decided to come back one last time to check if Peculiar was there. She came in the shop and peered around. Again, she saw no one. She looked all over the shop and saw the basement door wide open. She wanted to satisfy her curiosity and walked downstairs. The woman gasped as she saw all the dolls lying next to each other on the floor. She looked at each doll hoping to see the one that belonged to her, but she didn't. For some reason, it was not there. What she did see was a doll that resembled Mr. Newman Grace. She put her hands on her head and felt very faint. She went back upstairs and anxiously called the police. She didn't understand what had happened. The woman explained to the police that it might have been a robbery or even a kidnapping. Five minutes later, the police arrived. The two officers checked for evidence and did a full check in the basement. The two officers chuckled at the doll who had resembled Mr. Newman Grace but also wondered what happened to Peculiar. Even her house was empty and from the looks of it—a few weeks. Nothing was stolen from her home or the shop. This crime left everyone puzzled.

Two months had passed, and Mr. Grace's family just assumed he was dead. There was no body found and no sign of him anywhere. The town sheriff took over the department of health and made other arrangements for new rule in the town. A year later the shop had been remodeled after going into foreclosure. New owners bought the place along with the dolls. The dolls were placed in cube shelves in the back of the store. They were displayed so beautifully for all the customers to see. The owner picked up Fallow and looked at her with an evil smile. Her husband walked over to admire the doll too. They both looked at each other and shook their heads with pride. Fallow winked her eye to them, and they said, "Yes, we are doll lovers too."

The Boy Who Became
Mr. Elijah Whitman

It was Sunday and all the people that were in my group were ready for the preacher to come and speak on Monday. This was a religious group of people who believed in God and spent their pastimes staying far away from anyone who smoked cigarettes and cursed at their slutty daughters. I was part of that group. As sad as it sounds, I wish I had never revealed my secret of sin.

The sunshine peered happily through my bedroom window. On this day, September 23, was the first time in all my life that I felt such an urge of hate. It rumbled inside me like a bear waiting to get out of the zoo. My name is Dale, and I became my idol who is also my teacher. It began one day while I was sitting in my third period history class. This was the most boring subject ever. I'd always fall asleep during this time. The other students seemed very interested in the escapades of the 1800s. I, on the other hand, couldn't wait until the bell rang. I dozed off into a dream where I was being chased by this man who had long teeth and red eyes. His mouth was wide and gaping open with drool looking at me with hunger in his eyes. I woke up abruptly only to see my teacher staring in my face with his hands in the air.

"No sleeping in class, Dale, or you can chase your daydreams in detention!"

He was always yelling for the simplest reasons. I think somehow it gave him a hard-on. I shook my head and sat straight up in my seat. I opened my textbook and pretended to read. Detention was the last place that I had wanted to spend my Friday, and so with that, I forced myself to listen to the last thirty-five minutes of lessons. Finally, the bell rang, and I was heading to my favorite class of the day. Algebra and Calculus was an important part of my grade, but it was also the most endearing time because of my teacher, Mr. Elijah Whitman. Mr. Whitman was scribbling down some simple equations on the board for the class to practice. I admired him so much and his physical appearance was the only thing that I often fantasized about the most. My biological mother did lots of drugs when she was pregnant with me, and because of her addiction, I was left with the grotesque scar of beauty. Blah…I hated my face. I was slightly deformed for the rest of my life, but I was going to fix that soon enough. After class was over, I asked him what quizzes were going to be given after the weekend. He responded by saying that we were going to have a pop quiz on some exponents and calculus problems as well as some basic fractions. For a moment, I just stood there gazing into his eyes and imagining myself in his suit and tie. He snapped his fingers and asked me if I was okay.

I said, "Yes, I'm fine, sir, I'll see you on Monday." I walked out the front door of the school and went straight to the bike rack in the parking lot. I wanted to see if there were any bikes that was left by someone. For some reason, I had good luck last year. There was a blue speed bike left from a student who got transferred and never claimed it. That bike eventually broke down after a month though. I decided to walk home. The cool autumn breeze blew through my hair and my troubles seemed to vanish for a second. As I got to my front door, my adopted parents were already home early. They were the best thing that ever happened to me. They took me in once my mother overdosed when I was twelve and have been like my biological parents ever since. My mother, Alice, who was a very beautiful woman gave me a hug and kiss on the cheek. She was a thin woman with long, red hair. My father, Glenn, was a short, stubby man with an odd hairline. He often covered it with a toupee when he went out in public. It didn't make a difference to me, I would take that hairline any day over my appearance. My father was a banker and my mother was an accountant at this prestigious law firm. My father came into the dining area and tussled my hair.

"How was your day, son?"

"Oh, I was just waiting, Dad."

Every day I came from school they asked me the same question, and every time I gave them the same answer. They knew what I meant, and they were waiting too. I ate some of the stew that my mother had made for dinner. She kissed me on my forehead, and I went upstairs. I went into the bathroom to shower. I hated to see my ugly reflection, but I also couldn't avoid it either. I put on my pajamas and went into my bedroom. I was a monster, and the other person inside me carried on like a beast in my nightmares. I had to wait because if I let him come out too soon it would be so unperfect. I lay awake for a moment in my bed, thinking of how it was so difficult growing up with my biological mother. I never knew my father. I supposed he was a junkie too. I remember vaguely in kindergarten how the kids made fun of me. Some of them were often very frightened of me too. They cried heavy tears whenever my mother had dropped me off in the morning to school. Of course, I had expected a hug or some comfort from her, but I didn't realize the emotional detachment until I became an adolescent. After she overdosed on heroine, I was taken to at least six foster homes. I got lucky by living with the parents I'm with right now. They didn't care about how I looked, to them I was still special. The town I live in isn't much different from what I was used to. My mother had a house and a good job. She cleaned hotels for a living, and the pay was good, but once she became an addict, she lost everything. That's when we became homeless. The neighborhood is great. People still stare, but I accumulated a wide range of friends because my parents were so cool. I guess they felt sorry for me, so they basically let me throw parties and lots of the cool kids loved to come over. They didn't adapt well at first when I moved here, but once my father bought me that fire-red convertible, my popularity went sky-high. Who said money can't buy friends? After that my appearance never bothered them. My father bought me whatever I wanted, and they knew that. Sometimes I bought my friends drugs and booze. It was exciting for me. It was the only acceptance that I had right now. The girls never really wanted to date me. We had casual hookups and group get togethers at my house but nothing more. I imagined how sickening it must be to have sex with an ugly ogre. I called myself the guy from the Hunchback of Notre Dame. I was in high school and still a virgin. Other guys I knew stood around after class in the halls talking about which girl they wanted to screw and how their penis erupted two times after ejaculation. I couldn't even spell it. I guessed the feeling must have been marvelous. I watched rated R movies pretty often when I was alone and wanted to be comforted by the opposite sex. They were barely PG-13. The scenes were not that erotic but just the slightest scene of a woman undressing and showing a nipple was enticing for me. My eyes got heavy, and I thought of going to sleep. I slept for a few hours only to wake up to find a note from my parents. They told me they were at this Italian restaurant in town and they'd get a movie after. Lucky for them, I was alone again. I was tired of this. Tired of waiting and waiting, and I figured it was time. Time for me to stop being alone and finally live the life that I deserved and to be normal like everyone else. I stormed out of the house and walked to visit my favorite teacher. As I walked, I saw myself turning handsome and all the girls wanting to date me. I walked past a mailbox and saw a postcard that someone accidentally dropped on the ground. Curiously, I picked it up.

It read, "Hi, how are you, I never met a man so handsome in my life. I'm really glad you don't look like a monster or I never would have dated you. Just kidding. See you soon, xoxo."

He dropped the postcard on the ground hoping whoever dropped it would end up breaking up with their sweetheart. He felt pitiful and disgusted. Everyone in this world seemed to be concerned about who's the prettiest and fairest one of all. He felt like he was living in storybook surrounded by characters that were monsters themselves as soon as the light went out. Beauty is only skin deep, they say. Yeah right, the mere fact was looks were what made you who you were, and they determined his future and held no real promises. He finally arrived at Mr. Whitman's front door. He began to get nervous and the palms of his hands were drenched with sweat. He wiped his hands on the back of his jeans and rang the bell. He stood there for a moment waiting then a man answered the door. It was Mr. Whitman.

He had a puzzled look on his face and asked, "Hello, Dale, what are you doing here, forgot your textbook?" Mr. Whitman gave a chuckled laugh and stared at his student standing at his front door.

"No, I actually came to visit you, how are you today?" Dale smiled a crooked smile and looked intensely at his teacher.

"How about you come inside and tell me what's the reason for your visit." He invited Dale in and closed the door. Not realizing this would be the very last time he'd see life again as we know it. They walked to the kitchen area where Mr. Whitman was supposedly enjoying some crackers and wine. They sat at the kitchen table. Mr. Whitman stared long and hard at the boy. He asked him was he in some type of trouble. He was in trouble, trouble with being a gruesome thing. Wanting so badly to release the beast from within. He couldn't hold it in any longer. The boy began to twitch and squirm. His eyes rolled in the back of his head and returned to their sockets a fiery red. Mr. Whitman gasped in horror, fell back in his chair, and stumbled to the floor. Dale walked over to him, his teeth protruding from his mouth growing more, and more intense with hunger. He grabbed the teacher's legs and pounced on top of his body while pinning him to the floor. Still changing into this horrible creature, he stuck out his long tongue and began to suck the life out of Mr. Whitman's brains. *Slurp, Slurp, Slurp, Slurp.*

When Dale got home, his parents were already back from their brunch at the restaurant. They both looked at their son with huge happy eyes. His parents held hands and looked at each other and then looked at Mr. Whitman and said, "My, what a handsome young man you are."

Sally's World of Fairies

The wind blew on this fantastic morning. There was a whistle within the breeze. A sound that caught your ear and whispered a secret. The little people stayed in a distance. From a faraway land came creatures that healed a child's sadness and befriended their trust. After it was over, the reality of who they really were was discovered.

My name is Sally Woods. I met the beautiful creature on my way home from school. It flew into the sunlight and into my own existence. I thought my imagination was running wild again but this time I had seen it with my own eyes. A fairy. Not just any fairy, a pleasant one that sat on your left shoulder and buzzed in your ear like a mosquito. I walked a fast pace trying to get away, but it kept following me. I was scared and confused. I took the shortcut to my house and finally reached my front door.

"What are you in such a hurry for?" my mother asked me curiously.

My mother had a keen sense of when I was under pressure. Aside from breathing hard and small pearls of sweat trickling down my forehead, I managed to tell her I was running from the neighbor's dog. The one that got out of the yard again.

"Oh, well, I think I will call the ASPCA if the Martins refuse to keep him on a leash."

Margaret was an only child of one other sibling that died at birth. Her mother named her Margaret after their great-grandmother who was Irish. Didn't sound like an Irish name to me. So my mother preferred people to call her Marge. I went inside and dropped my book bag on the floor and ran upstairs to my room. I sat on the edge of my bed thinking and wondering to myself. I just turned thirteen. Was it even normal anymore to fantasize about things that seemed almost impossible? My mother told me that when my father died of a heart attack, she would dream of him being there. She said sometimes your mind could work up a fix of things when a tragedy occurs. Those are called hallucinations. This was no tragedy, I simply couldn't understand the awkwardness of it all. I took my clothes off and slid into my pajamas. It was nearly four o'clock now. I didn't feel like going to Rachel's house or anything. Rachel was my best friend since kindergarten. I just wanted to fall asleep and wake up hoping it was just a dream. Rachel would never know about this. This was one secret I wouldn't even tell her.

I woke up feeling very frustrated because it was the weekend. I spent a day of bonding from shopping with my mother. We often went down to the local doughnut shop and bought a dozen doughnuts with a caramel latte. *Mmm, I loved caramel lattes.* My mother said it was just a bunch of flavored syrup and mostly coffee. The caffeine wasn't good for me. She was addicted to coffee herself. It was a treat I rarely got, so whenever I did get one, I was happy. I heard the television set playing downstairs in the living room. Mom was a reality-TV-series type of person. Inheriting my father's benefits from his death left her with this boring life of what was real on TV and in reality. She became depressed but eventually took up a hobby of knitting. She made a small income on the side as her pastime job when she was bored or depressed. That she did very well.

"Hey, darling, how did you sleep?" she asked me as I walked into the kitchen.

I told her fine and opened the refrigerator and reached for the milk. I grabbed a bowl and spoon from the dish rack on the counter and sat at the table preparing a big bowl of cereal. My mother looked at me, the living room and kitchen were both adjacent in her view. I told her it was fine and went into the refrigerator and reached for the milk. I grabbed a bowl and spoon from the dish rack on the counter and sat at the table preparing a big bowl of cereal.

"It doesn't seem like you're feeling well, ever since you raced in here like a roadrunner," my mother said.

I took another spoonful of my cereal and looked up from my bowl.

"Well, if I asked you a weird question, would you think I was crazy?"

I stared at my mother and hoped she would say yes, so I wouldn't have to tell her in the first place.

"No, honey, you're my daughter, and whatever you're feeling, I'd like to know."

She looked at me with sympathy in her eyes. My mother was caring and also very convincing at times.

I shrugged my shoulders and said, "Oh, I just wanted to know the difference between a hallucination or reality."

My mother explained to me about wild imaginations. She told me that whatever I thought about during the day usually manifested itself in your dreams at night. That was hardly the case. I had finished eating and told my mother I understood. I wanted to believe that her advice helped me; otherwise, she would worry that something was wrong. I took my sweater off the hook hanging in the hallway. I decided to take a walk to the park. I grabbed the phone from the dining room table and walked out the door. I felt like I was going crazy. I wanted to think this was a dream, but deep down inside I believed what I saw was very real.

I walked through the small trail that was lined with broken rocks that had led me into the woods. I often took this shortcut because it was no one on this trail to distract my thoughts. I was in my own world. I liked being in my own world because I can be whatever I wanted to be. I walked for a few more minutes, and I began to feel very lightheaded. In a distance, I could see something flying toward me. I hated bugs and I usually got bit by ants whenever I passed these weeping willow trees before I got to the park. This time I didn't even think I could make it to the park. My head started spinning, and that bug was in a distance flying now was almost as close to my nose. It wasn't a bug though, it had thin wings and a small body with beady little eyes staring at me. I shrieked and fell to the ground. I guess the fell shook me back in place because I didn't feel dizzy anymore. It was a fairy. She had probably followed me, but if she had followed me, where was she hiding all this time? I got up and just stood there looking at her in amazement. She flew around my head and then she landed on my arm. I wasn't afraid anymore. I opened my hand, and she gently walked into the palm of it. Her little feet felt like small taps across my fingers. She was completely naked besides a clothlike dress made from leaves covering her. She stood as tall as a crayon in my hand. She had hair that was the darkest brown, and it draped down to her tiny, little shoulders. She walked all around my hand, touching my skin with her fingers. It tickled a bit, and I let out a laugh that made her jump. She tilted her head to the side and opened her mouth. She seemed to be chattering something, but her voice was so low that I couldn't hear her.

"My name is Sally," I said, and she shook her head. "What's your name?" I asked her, putting my face down to the level of my hand.

She pointed to a dandelion flower on the ground that was lying next to a twig. "Dandelion, so that's your name."

I looked around the woods and saw that it was getting dark. I walked the opposite way to go back home but ended up just circling back into the same direction. I waved my hand at her to make her go away but she kept following me. I started to panic more because I realized I was lost. I knelt down next to a tree and sat down crying. Dandelion flew around me and looked at me with her sad, little eyes. She flew up into the air, she stood there waiting for me to notice her, and I looked up and wiped my eyes. Ahead I saw the most beautiful thing I ever seen. It was a rainbow of light coming from the other end of the woods. I began to walk toward the light and the colors somehow hypnotized me. The fairy followed my every step. I reached the reflection of the light and saw a door that was open. I couldn't see what was inside because the light was so bright. I walked through the door. Maybe this could take me back home, I thought. The door closed behind me, and I began to fall down this long, narrow tunnel. I screamed and covered my eyes. The tunnel took me all the way down to a place that was not home.

I landed with a thump, the bottom was unusually soft. Dandelion was still there, just flying around my head. I got up and was happy I had worn long pants today, otherwise my legs would of been scraped up for sure. My sweater had torn just a little from the fall. I was beginning to feel tired and frustrated. I wanted all this to end and most of all I wanted to go home. It was way past lunchtime, and I worried that my mother would be expecting me. I dug into my pants pocket and pulled my cell phone. The power was completely dead. Now I was really screwed. The fairy flew toward me and shook her small finger to my face. I was starting to understand her gestures even though her voice was too low for me to hear. I smiled at her, and she gave me a smile back. I kept walking because that was the only thing left to do if I wanted to get out of here. I felt a sense of terror, the hollow tunnel grew dark, and a shadow appeared on the wall. It had wings as big as an eagle. I turned around, and to my own horror, I saw Dandelion. Not sweet and shy but large and disgusting. She was salivating from her mouth staring at me with huge green eyes. The scent that billowed the area was a stench I will never forget. She walked toward me. Closer, closer, closer. Her breath smelled like a sewer, and I cried like I was going to a hell I never about. She grabbed me with one strong hand. Spit dripping from her mouth ready to taste me like a scrumptious feast. I heard a sound, the sound of a phone ringing. It was my cell phone. How was it ringing when it was dead. At least that was I thought being in this nightmare made things exist my imagination. This seemed to save my life because the sound echoed through the entire tunnel. Frightening Dandelion. She dropped me from her hand and put her hands over her ears to block out the ringing sound. I ran and finally reached the end. She ran behind me faster and faster. I saw the light, and I made it out. I made it, I found my way out. Dandelion was at the end, but she couldn't go any closer to the light. Suddenly the tunnel closed and swallowed her up. I stood there with a blank look on my face astonished. I ran all the way home.

My mother answered the door and said, "Honey, you're back so soon?"

I looked at her with a puzzled expression. It seemed like I was gone for hours. I reached in my pocket and felt my cell phone. It was still broken. I told her I dropped it by accident on my way to the woods. She looked at me and smiled. I had to ask her and for no reason but was anxious to know what she thought.

I looked up and said, "Mom, do you believe in fairies?" She smiled, and when she opened her mouth, her teeth were discolored and rotten. Wings appeared out the ends of her shoulders. I screamed the most awful scream I could have ever. I cried louder, but no one could hear me. She opened her mouth to speak.

She grunted and said, "Yes, I believe in fairies too!"

The Girl with the Silver Locket

I came across this passage that I was reading in *The New York Times* newspaper. It was a very descriptive article from a young man named Michael who had stumbled across a stranger, who wasn't really a stranger at all.

I was driving home at 10:00 p.m. only because my stupid girlfriend had upset me with her assumptions. We'd only been together for six months. And already I was being accused of sleeping with the receptionist at the firm where I worked. The frost in the air was heightened and there was bitter fog surrounding the bare road. Colorado was one of the many states that went below freezing in the winter. I'm not even a cold-blooded person, maybe just lukewarm. I was heading toward the highway intersecting a narrow road that was leading to a small town fight off Colorado Springs. Driving late at night was one of the many hobbies I often did to clear my head when I was upset. It was something about the night air and the seemingly quiet roads that eased the tension. Although Stephanie was beautiful, she knew exactly how to get to me. Of course, I wasn't cheating. After seeing my mother go through three divorces and only half a million dollars left to her as collateral from my father, leaving her for a model-type blond was the last thing she cared about. I wasn't going to let that happen to me. This was my fourth relationship in two years, and I refused to let this be about something that could of happened that didn't. I was medium height with broad shoulders. I did fashion some good looks after my father but in comparison to his infidelity, that was one thing I did not. I shook my head from those issues because right now I was in the midst of dozing off. I wanted to drive another half a mile and then decided to turn around. I realized I was going way too fast, I had to slow down. So I pulled over to a side area that was covered with shrubs and broken branches. Looking ahead I saw a blurry light that gave me a bit of a headache from glancing at it. It was almost midnight, and I was feeling more tired. Suddenly the blurred light that I saw up ahead was starting to turn into a figure. Did my dozing off so quickly conquer my subconscious mind I squirmed my face and squinted my eyes. The figure was turning into a girl, a girl with a silver locket around her neck. My fear was coming into existence now, it was time for me to go. There were no other cars on the road but mine. Odd but hardly funny at this time of night, or should I say morning. I began to start my car and for some reason, the car wouldn't move. This was starting to feel like a moment in the twilight zone. My heart was beating, and my palms began to sweat. The figure that appeared to be a girl was beginning to move toward my car. I froze in motion. Maybe if I just stood still it would disappear, or maybe it wasn't even a girl just a figment of my imagination perceiving it to be one. I had to admit that the road was pretty dark, the only thing that was visible right now were my headlights and the unknown figure approaching me. In an instant, the figure was standing next to my window. I shook my head and hoped by closing my eyes for a brief moment that it would go away. I was so utterly horrified that I screamed loud as my poor voice can take me. Suddenly the figure disappeared. My hands were shaking, and I jiggled the keys back into the ignition. I prayed that this time it would start. The loud cranking sound of the engine roared, and I sped off from that road and drove until I reached home. Back with my girlfriend and her weird cheating assumptions, I was actually happy for this moment. I was happy to see her sleeping peacefully in the bed. Thinking maybe if I was home, I'd be sleeping too. This experience would have never happened to me but to someone else. I was getting more tired by the minute. My eyes sank low, and I drifted off to sleep.

The next morning, I felt like I woke up feeling like I had a hangover. I was confused and disoriented. Stephanie served me breakfast in bed and apologized for accusing me of cheating with the receptionist. She found out that the receptionist was actually in a relationship with another woman and didn't care for men at all, go figure. Now I had to clear my thoughts, I was hoping she wouldn't have a thing for Stephanie; she's seen my girlfriend before. That will be funny, vice versa. I shook my head and kissed my girlfriend, thanking her for the breakfast that she had made. She went back upstairs and let me enjoy my meal of toast, scrambled eggs, and some hominy grits with a tall glass of orange juice.

Before she headed upstairs, she turned and asked, "Where were you last night, I was worried?"

I gave her a perplexed look and said, "Just driving as usual."

She was satisfied with my answer because she knew my drives were long and intense after an argument. She didn't know what I had encountered, and I was surely not going to tell her. I stared at my eggs on my plate and took two bites along with my bacon and sipped some of my orange juice. I felt I should tell her, but it was only a matter of time that she would think I was crazy. I couldn't contain the feeling like I was just inhabited by a ghost. After I ate my breakfast, it was nearly an hour before I had to make it to work. I kissed my girlfriend goodbye and told her I was going into the office a little early to finish the paperwork from last week. She was in an internship program at a nearby college. She only worked part-time hours, so she had at least another hour or two to sleep. Lucky for her, I wished I could just sleep at my desk without getting fired. I got into my car and felt a sense of uneasiness. I drove out the driveway and tried to clear my head. My boss was very keen on these kinds of things, and I didn't want him to see me freaking out. This act of behavior in front of him will surely have cost me a trip to the psychiatrist. I parked my car in the parking lot. I glanced over my shoulder to make sure that I wasn't being followed again. This was crazy, I had to get over this. I rushed into my office not wanting to greet any of my former employees this morning. I was feeling terrible, and I wanted this day to be over very fast. My boss came in and said "good morning" while at the same time placing a stack of papers laying on my desk. I started on the first pile.

Lunchtime came abruptly, and I was feeling content that the day was almost over. I decided to walk to the small coffee shop near my job. A young-looking waitress came to take my order. I wanted something simple.

"I'll just have a small Caesar salad and a lemon-flavored water."

She nodded her head in agreement and left to get my food. The waitress arrived with my food since there wasn't much customers today it wasn't a long wait. I paid for my food, and she gave me my receipt. As I was enjoying the freshness of my salad, the lettuce crunching against my teeth, the girl appeared again. The figure was a dark mist like a shadow in the daytime air. She appeared even more lifeless from the time I had seen her yesterday. I was even able to see the locket around her neck more clearly besides it was dark at the time. She stood in midair, her feet not touching the ground. There was some people passing by, and I wondered why they hadn't noticed her. Was she a ghost? I still wondered that. I knew she was visible to me but now that I knew no one else noticed her. I scarfed down half of my salad and guzzled half of my water, taking my eyes off her appearance for just that moment. I thought it would be a good idea that my stomach was full if this was something I really had to swallow. I got up from my seat and as soon as I did that, the figure was gone. I went back to work, feeling a bit creeped out. This was weird, and I started to feel nauseated. I walked into my office barely reaching the door and fainted.

My head ached, and I felt drained of all my energy. I had awakened to a nurse standing over my head waiting to take my temperature.

"Why am I here?" I asked her, feeling very tired and weak.

She told me I had fainted, and my boss called an ambulance. Coming into the room was my girlfriend Stephanie. She had tears in her eyes and asked if I felt well enough to go home. The doctors checked all my vitals, and it was normal again. The TV was over my head next to my bed. The news was playing talking about a few snow flurries coming our way. Then the newscaster announced something so horrible that I dreaded even waking up. Local Colorado resident found dead after reported being missing near the Colorado Spring Area. Farrah Conway, twenty-year-old girl found brutally beaten by a wooded area near the highway of Colorado Springs. The only other identity that her relatives were able to recognize her was that she was wearing a silver locket around her neck.

WHAT I GOT FOR CHRISTMAS

I have a story to tell, and it's the type of story you'd remember for the rest of your life. It happened in December, the same month Christmas carols were being sung. Pies were made with love and lives were stolen on the night. The meaning of Christmas meant a lot to me. I looked at the world differently then. I promised myself for as long as I lived that I would never, ever ask for a car for Christmas again. Winter came so suddenly, I was hoping it would snow in January, but luckily for all the people who really followed holiday tradition, it snowed on Christmas. You'd think as far as tradition went I'd be happy about that, but not having a car was worse. Bad enough I had to hitch rides with my friends and parents all the time. The Christmas tree stood in the far end corner in the living room. It looked as beautiful as it did last year. All the ornaments dangling from end to end. I was sixteen, and I also had my license. I was a senior in high school, and I wanted so bad for Sinclair to notice me. She dated mostly college guys and one football player. My name was Malcolm, and I had an average look. I had dark-green eyes and blond hair. My dress style was punk and even though I wasn't the most popular guy in school, the girls loved it. I had sort of a bad boy reputation, so I did fit in. It was like I was the only one in high school without a car. I lived in a big house right at the borderline of Southwest Beach. Our house paved the view of the ocean. In the winter, the beach was completely dry. My parents were split-up for the past seven months. My father tried to overlook my mother's selfish ways, and my mother tried to forgive him for cheating with his accountant. Two months ago, he purchased a tennis bracelet. She thought it was very generous of him, but they were married, and if I knew one thing was that marriage was supposed to be sacred. I often thought how dumb it was if two people were supposed to be in love and still cheat. What was the infatuation for all that—just be single. This was my last year before I graduated. My father was very proud of my progress and promised to get me exactly what I was waiting for. My father had a successful occupation in stocks and his trade with the marketing business went pretty well for someone who began his idea with a detailed blueprint. Being the child of a wealthy father had its advantages, but I was satisfied with simple stuff. My mother looked at me and nudged my shoulders out of my daydream.

"I want you to go and clean the garage, so I can start donating the stuff to the shelters downtown." Patty was a mother anyone could grow to love.

It was six in the evening; my father and I were heading downtown to get some Christmas decor and tons of cars were lined behind each other on the crowded highway. The scene was so intense—passengers and some drivers fumed with impatience from the accident up ahead. A woman and her daughter had been totally crushed by a hit-and-run driver, leaving the both of them sloppily sprawled out onto the ground. Blood had formed into a neat puddle surrounding the child's head. The little girl was just turning eight years old. Her mother was driving to her grandparent's house to celebrate. There was an officer dressed in a blue coat and black top hat. He was identified as Officer Raymond from the name tag pinned to his jacket. He walked quickly to all the cars and explained what had occurred during the accident. The mother's body was lifeless, and her neck was turned the other way. What a horrible way to die. I figured it happened so suddenly she probably didn't feel the pain. The little girl had suffered a broken spine and a head injury cracking her skull from the impact when she hit the window. It was only five more days until Christmas, and a tragedy had already ignited sparks of sadness before the holidays. The driver, who had caused the accident, had been caught trying to exit the nearest turnpike. He was handcuffed and arrested on the scene. Police were paired throughout the highway and yellow tape padded the area. We sat in the minivan for at least an hour. I was restless and tired. Soon after an officer up ahead waved an orange glow stick which directed the vehicles to proceed in the other direction. As my father began to drive out off the highway, we caught a glimpse of the vehicle that was in the accident. It was a 1973 cherry-red Corvette. The car was completely demolished. That was exactly the car I had wanted, maybe not the same model, but it was. We had finished shopping and were pulling into our driveway. My mother was standing in front of the door to greet us. She had heard about the accident on the radio. I got out and took the bags out of the trunk. My father got out and rubbed his head, walking side by side into the house with my mother. From the looks of it, he won't be going home tonight. The intersections were blocked off. I closed the trunk and carried the bags inside. Before I stepped in my front door, I saw a mist in the figure of a person. Then I suddenly realized it was a girl. I thought it was my neighbor's kid frolicking around, but it was too late for any child to be outside this time of night. It got dark around 8:00 p.m. I felt a cold chill brush beside me.

"Man, it's cold," I said.

I went inside and quickly forgot about it. I sat the bags in the kitchen on the floor and stood there for a moment watching my mother unpack. I went into the living room and saw that my father was comfortably asleep on the sofa. I spotted a glass of gin beside him on the end table—I guess that did it. I went upstairs to my bedroom and then showered. It felt good to finally lay in my bed after a long day. I felt a bit of sadness for that young girl and her mother. I started to see why it was so important to cherish your day like it was your last.

The last four days had come in very quickly. I went downstairs smelling freshly baked biscuits and sausages my mother had been cooking. My mother was always preparing big, hearty breakfasts on Christmas morning, followed by her homemade gingerbread cookies baked with love.

"Good morning, son, Merry Christmas."

I kissed her on the cheek. She was almost finished preparing the sausages. There was another skillet on the back burner cooking my favorite omelet with cheese, green peppers, and ham.

"Your father is coming to spend Christmas with us, can you believe it! Oh, and he said he has a very special gift for you too." my mother looked at me and winked her eye.

I smiled at the thought of what it might be. I helped her set the table for breakfast, and we both sat down and began to eat. After taking a few bites of my eggs, my mother poured us both a glass of orange juice.

I said, "I feel so strange about that accident we saw. It is really starting to make me feel crazy!"

My mother looked at me with concern in her eyes.

"What is this feeling maybe sadness or because it was near the holidays?" She took a bite of her sausage and waited intensely for my answer.

"I uh…well, it's just that, I don't know… I could have sworn I saw that girl the night me and Dad got back home."

I finished the rest of my eggs and took a long sip of my orange juice. My mother continued to eat her biscuit; after swallowing the last piece, she said, "Honey, that is pretty strange, but I've heard of these things happening to people that experienced visual traumas."

She looked at me again with concern in her eyes. They both continued to eat the rest of their breakfast in silence.

The evening was calm, and my mother played melodic Christmas carols on the record player. Afterward she played Frank Sinatra. She swayed to the melodies of his voice, prancing around the living room floor. The tree looked very colorful, and there were eight gifts total under it followed by a small saucer of gingerbread cookies sitting on an end table. A slight breeze blew in from the living room window. I glanced over in that direction, and I saw her again. I stood there frozen with fear, my heart fluttered in my chest, and my fingers had suddenly gotten numb. My mother didn't notice or probably couldn't see. In that moment, I realized she couldn't see what I saw. The doorbell rang, and I jumped. The girl suddenly disappeared. I looked around to see where she had gone, but my mother was already greeting my father at the door.

"Merry Christmas, son!" He had two perfectly wrapped presents tucked underneath his arm.

It was a big gold ribbon tied around each of them. I took the gifts and placed it under the tree. My father removed his coat and hat and neatly hung it on the coat rack behind the front door. He sat on the sofa and let out a huge, tired sigh. My mother stood there with a big smile on her face. For once in a long time, she seemed happy. What better way to engage in this moment with family on the holidays. My mother had prepared potato salad, pumpkin pie, and ham smothered with cranberry sauce. She gestured for us to come into the kitchen to eat before we sat down to open our gifts. My father reached into his pants pocket and took out a set of keys. He handed it to me. My father looked at me with wide eyes and a huge smile.

"Is this what I think it is, Dad?"

I enjoyed my Christmas dinner and immediately ran out the house expecting my surprise to be there, and it was. My mouth was gaped open with astonishment. The surprise I've been waiting for and he knew, he knew all along. The color was a freshy coated cherry red, and it was absolutely flawless. The girls and guys in my school were going to envy me all the way through college. I felt a tear of happiness fall from my eyes. I opened my mouth to speak, but I couldn't, my expression was enough thanks. Both of my parents were standing outside and began to huddle around me. They watched me with such joy as I rubbed my hands over the sleek surface.

After my sympathetic moment, I asked my father, "Dad where did you find this model it looks like the same one from that accident?"

"Son, when they made Porsche did they make just one?"

His father had explained how he had gotten this at a dealership, and they sold it to him for a thousand bucks. It was unreal but he took it.

"I got lucky."

This was luck all right, bad luck for sure. They went back inside and started to open the gifts that were under the tree. This was turning out to be a wonderful Christmas. Eating Mom's pie and drinking eggnog. Frank Sinatra played all night. I fell asleep on the sofa, and when I woke up, I saw that my parents weren't downstairs. I crept upstairs to go to my bedroom and peeked in my mom's room.

Cuddled up together were my parents sound asleep. I went into my own bedroom and went to sleep too.

Morning came, and my father was already at the kitchen table enjoying a cup of coffee with my mother.

"Hey, did you sleep well?" he asked.

I nudged his shoulder and glanced at my mother.

"I see you slept well too, Dad."

"Your father has some news to share. We aren't getting divorced," my mother said happily.

I was so happy that we were a family again. There was absolutely nothing that could spoil this moment. I got two things for Christmas that I didn't expect, but I never knew the worst was yet to come. We had a week out of school following New Year's. I thought of calling up a few friends to celebrate my precious gift, but I wanted to wait until I went back to school to show off. I wanted to take this time to lavish in the pleasure for myself. It was ten o'clock and I was already dressed and ready to go. My parents were glad, so that they were able to spend some quality time together. I opened the front door of my car and sat down in the plush leather seat. The feeling was amazing. I wore my red sports jacket and Louis Vuitton scarf to accentuate this fine, beauty of mine. I pulled the keys from my pocket and started the engine. The sound was satisfying, and as I pulled out of the driveway, I felt like a million bucks—literally. It was a calm Saturday morning, and I was going to enjoy every bit of it. I drove out of my neighborhood and stopped at the first light. A blond-haired girl sitting in the passenger seat with whom I guessed was her mother, winked at me. I smiled and continued to bask in my ego. I drove off fast and left the girl, four cars behind me. I stopped at a small café to have some breakfast. I was thankful for my father's expenses. My allowance was a fair amount. Since I was staying at home until I went to college. I didn't have to get a job right away. I parked my car in front of the small café and hopped out. I found an empty seat at the back. I sat down and picked up the menu. That was sitting on the table next to the salt and pepper shakers. I scrolled down to sandwiches and decided to try the egg and ham on light toast with home fries and a glass of orange juice. The waitress who was a middle-aged lady came over to my table and waited for me to speak. I told her I'd have the morning special, and she scribbled my order on a small pad with a pencil. Another waitress approached my table as she was leaving and bought me a glass of water. While I waited, I looked out of the window and saw that fucking girl again. I couldn't believe it, and I started to think, crazily that she was after me. The waitress returned to my table with my food, and I jumped up when she sat the tray on the table.

"Are you all right?" she asked.

"Yeah, just got a lot on my mind," I told her.

That was more than correct. I did have a lot on my mind now, wondering if I was experiencing some kind of hallucination or just going crazy. I stared at my food for a minute then picked up my sandwich. I took five big bites. I stuffed two mouthfuls of home fries down my throat. I swallowed hard and finished off my glass of orange juice. I was ready to leave, and the whole situation gave me a throbbing headache just thinking about it. I slid my hand into my pocket and took out a twenty-dollar bill and left it next to my tray for the waitress. I couldn't believe this was happening. I had to get a grip, or I might have fainted right there. I walked out the café and hurried to the car. I didn't know what to think or do. My heart was racing a mile a minute. I wanted to tell someone. I needed to know why this was happening to me. After I pulled off and was halfway on the highway, I heard a dragging sound coming from underneath my car. Now I was really getting upset. First, I go crazy with these stupid visions and now my brand-new car wants to malfunction. I pulled on the side of the road and got out. I went on the left-hand side and bent down on my knees to see if something was caught underneath the hood. Nothing. I thought for sure I had lost my mind. Maybe I needed to go home and rest. So I got back in my car and started driving again. *Clunk, clunk, drag, drag.* The sound started again. By now I had already gotten so frustrated that I banged my head on the steering wheel sounding the horn. I decided not to get out this time, just driving to Howard's Motors and Parts. I wanted him to check and see what the problem was. Hey, I wasn't a mechanic; maybe there was something going on underneath my car. I stopped in front of the motor shop and quickly got out of the car. I felt a bit disoriented and thought maybe, just maybe, having this car was starting to feel like a bad idea. A fat sloppy-looking man who was Howard, the owner, walked toward me. His expression was confused walking while his body flopped from side to side. He wore denim overalls with a long-sleeved shirt. His forehead was smeared with sweat, and I could see the perspiration spots underneath his shirt as he lifted his arms waving to me. Howard gestured for me to come inside, and I desperately walked into the shop. The shop was fairly large and there were six men working on cars that were all cranked up with some leverage tool. There was an office that was in a room adjacent to the sign that said restroom. In the office was a desk with two chairs and some papers scattered on top of it. A pen holder stood upright with a black telephone sitting beside it. I sat in one of the chairs while Howard sat at his desk facing me with a puzzled look on his face. He looked at me like I was familiar to him, his head tilting to the side as if to recognize me from somewhere else.

After sizing me up, he said, "Hey, boy, ya father name Calvin Theodore? 'Cus if it is, you sure as hell looks like him"

"Yeah, that's my dad, and what is it to you?"

He stood up from his chair and peeked out the small window that was in the corner of his office. He stared out for at least two minutes then put his attention back to me.

"Well, I see he gave you that fine car I sold him for Christmas. It runs really nice, don't it?" he said, looking nervously around the room.

"As a matter of fact, I came in to see you because it doesn't run well," I told him.

"Okay, I can take a look at it." Both guys went outside, and Terrence watched as the fat guy put a rubber mat underneath the car.

He called on of his workers to crank up the car so he could see what was going on. He plopped down on the mat and it made a farting sound as he lay down to view the vehicle. He took a flashlight from his pocket and squinted his eyes. Trying to see if he saw anything under the wheels. There was nothing there. How strange was that. He got up and out the flashlight in his pocket.

"Well, I don't see anything, boy, maybe you must have ran over something."

He touched the pressure of the wheel and shook his head. Terrence stood there bewildered and thought if he had hit something, he would have surely felt the pressure from the hit. He marched back inside the shop and looked angrily at Howard.

"Mister, you said you sold this car to my father right, so how could you possibly not know if something was wrong with it?"

Terrence stood looking at the mechanic with his hands folded across his chest. Howard sat back in his seat and pulled the chair to his desk.

He looked at Terrence and explained, "You see, this shop here is where we fix and sell used cars. This car was bought into my shop all smashed up around December 20, just recently, yeah."

People told me to destroy it because it was damaged so bad from some accident but it's worth a lot of money. I got a great insurance deal from it and invested half that money into my new shop that's going to be built next year. Terrence felt a whip of heat brush against his face. Small white spots began to circle above his head. He felt lightheaded and faint. His heart started pounding a mile a minute. He figured out the reason why he had seen that girl and why he had heard that clunking sound underneath his car. It was when that accident happened, the officers had told us her body was dragged on the road. She had died a sudden death. I heard an old folk's tale that when you die suddenly that your spirit may still be wandering. The impact was so sudden that she probably don't know she's dead. I felt myself drift into a deep sleep and my body was drifting off the floor. When I woke up, I was in my bedroom, and I saw my parents. They were grinning at me with a devilish smile on their faces. My father had an eerie look on his face while staring down at me. He was dangling the keys in my face to the cherry-red car.

He said, "I have a surprise for you, son." I got up from my bed, not remembering how I got there.

I walked outside and saw the cherry-red Corvette in the driveway. I stared real hard and long at the car. I saw what I didn't want to see. Sitting in the seat was my mother, and in the passenger seat was that girl. I dozed off into another daydream and let my body float off into non-existence. Be careful what you ask for, because you just might get it.

About the Author

Yolanda Acker began writing poetry when she was in middle school and eventually converted her poems into short stories. She always admired the excitement of horror, so she started adding plots and twists that allowed her short stories to become her main hobby. She began writing her first short story "The Haunting of Addie Longwood" in 2009, followed by other various short stories. The genres range from horror to suspense to sci-fi fantasy. She was born and raised in Brooklyn, New York, but moved to Connecticut to raise her five children. She is also a teacher to her homeschooled children as well as a writer. Yolanda is currently pursuing to further her education with an online course in law as a paralegal. She chooses to work from home as a virtual paralegal while obtaining her career as an author.

www.ingramcontent.com/pod-product-compliance
Lightning Source LLC
LaVergne TN
LVHW041548060526
838200LV00037B/1198